BECOMING AN
INCREDIBLE WOMEN

In The Midst of Your Storm

TEMIKA MCCANN

COPYRIGHT

DEDICATION

I would love to first give honor to my LORD and savior Jesus Christ. I want to dedicate this book to my Companion Johnny L.H. My beautiful five daughters Shartis, Brionna, Malaya, Kyla, and Janiyah. Also to my lovely parents Judy. B. Lonzo and Willie E.M. My grandmother Mama Ruth M. and Grandfather Johnny M.

Special thanks to my uncle "Pastor W.E. Page", "John H", "God – Mother Mary Bowen", "Mitchell Fletcher", "Lisa Rhodes", "Jennette Anderson", "Joe Bailey", "Joyce Predom", "Renee McCann friends", "Uncles, Aunties", "Nephews", "Nieces J. Smooth", "my Godbrother Prophet James", "Angela Roberson", "Jai", "Michael", "Mesha, Vina", and a host of family and friends for supporting, encouraging and believing in me. May God bless you!

P.S. If I miss anyone charge it to my head and not my heart!

Table of Contents

INTRODUCTION

Life never seems to roll along, smooth and calm, at least not for everyone and not for long. People that seem to have it all today have a life experience that comes with their achievements. As for me, I do feel like I have had my unfair share of difficult times in life. We might not often see our times of difficulty in life as blessings in hindsight. However, experience had made me realize that there is light at the end of the tunnel if we are willing to see the end of it.

I grew up in the Inter-City; it was a lovely experience growing up with both parents, raised with the proper values and morals of life. I was the third child with four adorable sibling Vincent, Mario, Lonzo Jr, Brandon. We all lived and standard life happy and contented with what we have got. My dreams and expectations in life were like any other ambitious and goal getting American girl. To finish my high school, go to college, get an excellent job, marry the love of my life, have beautiful kids and live happily ever after.

I was making efforts devotedly towards achieving my goals and dreams in life. I already knew how to be responsible at the age of thirteen, and I got my first job. Life was going on pretty okay until the 'unexpected' happened. I was just sixteen, about to become a senior in high school, I was not conscious of my time of the month, and I had some strange feelings. You probably guessed right; I was pregnant. As a teenager and still in high school with all of life's ambition and goals lying ahead, I was overwhelmed at the realization of my teenage pregnancy. I felt the whole world has ended for me and probably that would have been the best time I wished the world will come to an end. It was a terrible feeling. How was I going to cope? How would I be able to graduate from high school, talk-less of going to college? How would my family take the news? How would society and other students at school see me? I was still young, still under the care and protection of my parents, still learning about life's struggles and challenges; it should not be me that this was happening to.

As if being pregnant at a very young age was not enough, with all the fear and anxiety that had suddenly crept into my life, I had to visit the doctor. My baby was going to be a girl, and sadly the doctor told me that she was going to have a rare disability. This news brought in another layer of devastation for me. It all became more complicated for me to understand and I blamed myself for her condition. I felt embarrassed; I felt ashamed. I felt sad, I felt irritated. The feelings were sometimes indescribable. I felt like giving up on everything, my dreams, my goals, my future. Nothing was particular about my life anymore. I had disappointed a whole lot of people because I was raised in a great home, where respect, values, and morale were very vital lessons for us to live our everyday life.

My mother was furious at the news of my pregnancy. I can still remember her telling me that "It is only one QUEEN in this house and you will have to finish your school." After hearing this statement from my mom, it motivated me into a position to become all that I will not be. Yes, it had happened, no going back on this. I became a teenage mom while still in high school, but yet I was always determinate to finish my high school and look forward to graduating at the appropriate time regardless of becoming a young mother. I did not allow my teen pregnancy to define who I was as a person. In the midst of all the turmoil and negative situations, I faced with and the enormous responsibility that was upon me being so young. As reality kicked in, I realized that it was going to be an easy task. However, I did not know that this was building the incredible woman inside of me in the midst of the storm I was facing. So many people always look at me as being a bright, strong and courageous young woman and still up to now, but did not realize the fears and storms I was battling on the inside of me.

I had always being a determined person and always wanting to become an incredible woman no matter what, I was going through. I felt like all through my life I had to fight harder than others to accomplish everything that I have. All of these trials and tribulation was building an incredibly strong woman inside of me. I had to realize that storms come to make you into who you are. To shape, form and mold you into becoming an incredible woman that I had always desired to be. What these storms did to me was to become this incredible, I continue to remain open-minded, positive, focused, determination, effort, commitment and accountability from family and friends. I was focusing on finishing high school and planning to graduate at the age of seventeen. With all the support I could get from my family and educators that believed in me, I was able to accomplish my goals.

Finally, I had my child, motherhood is such a great experience and comes with loads of responsibilities. I felt like I would not be able to go to college because I had to take up two jobs to provide for my child and me. So many responsibilities for me at a very young age, I had to pay my mom for child care and help put as much as I can to support the house with the little income I was getting both from work and welfare. All of these got me to where I needed to be, but I did not want to rely on welfare for the rest of my life, so I knew I had to further my education. At the age of 19, I had to make a sound decision to either remain on welfare and work my two jobs or continue my education to support my disability child.

As if my life was not already complicated enough, in the midst of all I was going through, becoming a teen mom; having a child with a disability; had two jobs, I got pregnant the second times. At this point, my dreams of ever going to college were becoming only a figment of my imagination. I was asking myself how I will finish school now with two kids. However, I had to build up my courage; nothing was going to stop me from achieving all my goals. I had to adjust my schedule to complete all that I had despite all the opposition that was coming my way, but through it all, I was still going to become this incredible woman I wanted to become. I did not allow my second pregnancy to stop me from going back to school, although insecurity crept in my life and feeling inadequate.

I felt like I had failed again. I became an enemy to my self did not realize that all these issues were yet building that incredible woman inside of me. I still was battling in my mind until I stop believing in myself and felt like how will I finish school now with this greater responsibility, but I continue to go to school. I did not quit; I am so grateful by the grace of GOD for the support of the father of my child John. L.H. and my mother consistently.

I finally graduate with my A.A. degree; I start feeling my courage coming back. I became very fearful all of the sudden of returning to school, I kept speaking to my inner man positive affirmations I said, "I can do this" , "I am a winner," and I am more than a CONQUER, and I found myself enrolling in school to get my B.S. Degree in Early Childhood. After graduating I had a total of five children, and now I had a greater responsibility. For me to take care of all my children now, I discover how vital education was. My grades were going down; I was very nervous. I felt like how can I get a Master Degree, Am I not smart enough even after me accomplishing two other degrees? I had a great support team that

6

believed in me. Even with all the fears that I was facing deep down inside I never gave up on my dreams.

In this book, you will see how this valuable information has changed my life and cause me to become this incredible woman in the midst of the storm and despite all the obstacle that I was facing. To conquer the storm, you have to make sure that you put in a lot of efforts and face who you are and whom you want to become. For this and many unspoken reasons, please do not tell me you cannot achieve your goal; please do not tell me you are tired; please do not tell me that it is impossible to become the person you want to become. You are born to win; you are born to succeed if you decide to live life without excuses. You owe yourself at least a trial, and then if you tell me that you cannot, I will show you how you can. I know how because I have walked the path; I had experienced many things in life, probably the same thing you are experiencing right now; I have been in your shoes but thank God yours might not be as bad as what I had to go through to get to where I am today.

Join me as I walk you through the path of success. Enjoy!

CHAPTER 1

LEARN A MORAL LESSON FROM EXPERIENCES

People often believe that the way our lives unfold is pre-determined by a higher power; that our trials and tribulations are tests or lessons that have been laid out before us and are beyond our control. Whatever it may be, I like to believe that although hardships and sorrow are sometimes beyond our control, every experience is valuable and leading us somewhere beautiful. Look at me today, from a teenage mom still in high school to become a woman that other people look up to and value the experiences I had to go through in life.

I believe there are happy endings, but sometimes we have to look farther inward so that you might see them. It can be tough to understand when you're in the midst of a crisis; trust me, I've been there. However, from my current vantage point, in a moment of grace, I see that I've always survived. Whatever it was, the final takeaway was a vibrant, fertile experience that has created who I am today. Moreover, for that, I wouldn't change a thing. So what are the things that a down moment in one's life can teach us?

Experiencing things that you don't want makes you clear about what you want: It's like research; some experiments work out, and some don't, but you're still gathering data the whole time. When something we don't like what happens to us, we know we want the opposite and vice versa. With hard times comes amazing clarity.

Challenging life experiences give you more empathy for others: It's incredible when people often tell me about things they're going through, and I'm able to relate. Depression, anxiety, yes, I can relate because I have been there. That is one side of having experienced a lot of hardship and challenging times in just about my life. I now have a wellspring of quality experience to share with others and motivate. I'm sure you have your own skills as well that you might not even really know.

You will appreciate whatever you have the more when the going finally gets good: Before I got pregnant as a teenager, things were nice and cool but I never really valued all that, until when I had to struggle through life to become what I am today. Now I have love, family, friends, and work that fulfills me, but I have felt the pain of going through the storms of life to get all these things. The experience of a storm can deepen your sense of gratitude, "The deeper that sorrow carves into your being, the more joy you can contain."

You are always stronger than you realize: I have experienced situations where I thought I could not possibly pull through and yet I did. Moreover, I did not only survived, but I also thrived. We as human beings are stronger than we give ourselves credit for, and that provides us with the confidence needed to face whatever new challenges lie ahead. Just like I became pregnant the second time, I felt it was all over, but I pulled through.

The survival tools you develop during hard times; stay with you for life: I've developed tools to utilize whenever times get tough again, which they always will, it's all just part of the natural flow of life. When I find myself in tough circumstances, pushed to the brink and grasping for any shred of joy, I will reach for relief in small moments of beauty and grace because I know that there will be happiness at the end of it all.

All we need are steps to help reconnect to our true self, and it is pure unconditional love and joy despite whatever it is we may currently be experiencing. That is our life's work. If we never had hard times, we wouldn't have an opportunity to work harder.

CHAPTER 2

DON'T GIVE UP SO EASILY

Almost everybody hits a particular stage in their lives where they are confronted with the alternative of either engaging on or surrendering. It may be the case that you were running a race and all you wish to do is quit running, or it may be the case that you have been pursuing your goals and dreams and it appears as if it will take forever. Times like this, individuals need to discover a hold that they never knew they had and see the inspiration to battle on to the end goal. On the off chance that you at any point had a craving to give up and you required motivation to continue, here are some great reasons why you ought to never surrender.

Good things in life don't come that simple: The most comfortable feat on the planet is lounge around and be lethargic and not attempt to accomplish anything. However, we as a whole realize that the absolute best things in life are the ones that are hard to achieve. Regardless of whether it's battling your way to the highest point of the stepping stool, or through the ups and downs of a long separation relationship; it may be difficult, however despite all the trouble, the prizes will be justified at the end of it all.

If You Give up Easily, You'll Ponder on what could have happened if you'd gone ahead: If you quit early, you will never know without a doubt regardless of whether you could have made it and that will play at the forefront of your thoughts for whatever remains of life. A few things that we set out to accomplish, we get one shot at, along these lines, if you don't see it to the finish, you may never get another chance at it.

In the Actual Fact, Instant Success those not exist: For many great people, an accomplishment in any field of attempt requires significant investment and diligence, and there will be obstacles in route. Sportsmen and ladies need to prepare hard, and they don't win each race, even entertainment superstars and successful business people we all see today most of them started at the bottom. The ones who are at the highest point of their diversion are the ones who pushed to the end and never surrendered.

On the off chance that you quit now, you could be setting a limiting point of reference for the future: The issue with stopping is that surrendering can turn into a propensity since you begin to trust that you will never have the capacity to prevail at anything. Then again, that is likewise why a few people appear to have the ability to win at all that they put their egos too. It isn't so much that they are great at everything; it's that they never surrender, and they have the propensity for winning.

Probably you haven't discovered the correct approach towards your goals yet: Succeeding is typically a procedure of experimentation. A cook may change his formula ordinarily before he hit only the right flavor blend, and as we all know, a government official may change his perspective occasionally, to get enough votes! The bottom line is that they don't surrender or give up at the first attempt, they might have just changed their approach, and afterward, they attempt once more.

Just doing "all right" never shows signs of changing anything: People endeavor to accomplish things since they need to roll out improvements, either to possess lives or for the advantage of other individuals. Giving up might be the most simple alternative to take and, for some time, you may feel soothed that you quit. At last, you will likely lament that choice because you're stopping will imply that all the exertion you put in was squandered and you didn't make any impact.

The main disappointment will be that you gave up without a fight: If you give all that you have to accomplish something regardless of getting the outcome that you sought after, you are not a washout since you gave a valiant effort. A minor nation may have just a single contender entered in the Olympics with zero chance of winning by any stretch of the imagination. However, the world will commend that individual as a champ since they drove forward and they didn't stop, the same applies to every point of life.

The last couple of miles are dependably the most disturbing miles: At the start of a venture, individuals are generally all started up and prepared to go, it's towards the end that they come up short on steam, lose intrigue, and they start to surrender. The last extent is dependably the hardest, however that is precisely the time that you shouldn't quit since you have come up until now. See it to the finish, and you will be glad that you didn't stop.

You will end up motivating other individuals: If not for yourself, at that point consider the general population you could stimulate by your not surrendering. Via going ahead, against the chances, you could motivate your kids, your family and companions, and even entire outsiders, not to abandon their particular battles.

You will inevitably regret giving up: One of the most significant motivations why you should not surrender is that you likely think twice about it on the off chance that you do. You get one shot at life, and many possibilities tag along once, so confront the difficulties head-on and see them to the finish. On the off chance that you don't, you will be perpetually pondering on what it could have been had you not surrendered.

CHAPTER 3

DON'T LET EXCUSES DEFINE YOU!

I had all the excuses I needed in the world to give up on my dreams when I first got pregnant at the age of sixteen. Even when I got to know that my child was with a disability, I got another round of excuses to give. I struggled to complete high school; I got pregnant again, which brought the reason not to go to college.

As far as I can remember since I was a young girl and up to now, I have always encountered major storms ranging from internal, external, mentally, physically, socially and emotionally. I had gone through storms in life that were very devastating but survived through it all. I survived every storm with the help of the Lord and a good strong support team that believed in me. You might be saying how did you survive your storms? How did you not let these storms become an excuse in your life? I am so glad you ask. I did it through prayer, fasting, focus, and determination. Storms can come in many forms: death, rejection, loss of job, relationship, up and downs in life, mental break downs and sickness and the list can go on and on.

I had to realize that life comes with struggles, troubles, and disappointments, you can choose to wallow in your storms, but you will never develop into the incredible person that you wish to be without facing each storm head-on. We all have storms that will rise in our lives at any giving time. What we need to realize is that it's not the storm, but it is your perception on how to come out of the storms rather than focusing on the storms that you are facing, put more of your focus on the solution. I have discovered that focusing on your storm will cause you to miss out on all the incredible outcome that life has to offer. I now can look back over all my challenges in life that now allowed me to develop into the incredible women and to be able to help other women along with their journey. Challenges bring out the very best in you and sometimes it is hard to see because we are so focused on the pain. I am grateful that now I understand that to develop into an incredible person that I had always wanted to be, I had first to allow myself to look within and speak hope into my challenges in life.

I want to encourage you as I had to learn to promote myself. I have no clue of the nature of the challenges that you might be facing nor the magnitude, but what, I can say with God, strategies, the right resources, networking with others who might be facing the same issues you are, strong support team and people holding you accountable for your actions and the support of family and friends, there is no storm that you can never face. With effort and perseverance, you can overcome it and develop into that dynamic, incredible women that you have always was intended to be.

Life will provide you with excuses: It's your choice to take it or leave it. As for me, I left all those excuses behind. I didn't let that define whom I was going to be in life. You also have that choice to make, and it is essential to know that the excuses we make regularly prompt stagnation and life of disappointments. Besides, achievement in any field of undertaking requires a time of inconvenience where we should wander into new aspects of our lives that prompt unexpected situations. Remember all these things as I walk you through how you don't let excuses define who you are.

Don't Compare Yourself To Others: Comparing yourself with other people will regularly influence you to feel dampened, mainly when you can't meet up to some individuals' benchmarks of accomplishments. Ideally, it would be best if you only compared yourself with yourself when you are at your best. No other person is required. On the off chance that through your most astounding endeavors you outperform your own best; that is the point in your life that you need to always make as a point of reference until you achieve another outstanding moment in life.

Avoid Dwelling on the Past: The minute we start dwelling on past errors or disappointments is the minute we begin encountering the feeling of failure. Rather than assuming liability for our choices and activities, we instantly hope to blame somebody or another thing for justifying our failures. Accordingly, we defend and rationalize our fizzled endeavors.

Given this, try to focus on the present minute instead of on your past. Indeed, gain from your missteps and disappointments, yet don't utilize them as a stage for your reference book of excuses.

Focus on Solutions and Opportunities: When we make excuses, we regularly center on issues, laments, and on things that didn't work. To kill reasons from your life, you should instead start concentrating on arrangements, openings, and on the things that did work. It's a necessary move, yet if we keep this standard at the front line of our brain while rationalizing; it will quickly change our viewpoint of the current circumstance.

Seek Alternate Perspectives: Frequently, the excuses we make are a consequence of an absence of point of view. We don't have or comprehend the master plan. It resembles looking through a keyhole. You will never observe the whole room; just a little segment of that room.

Say for example you looked through a keyhole and saw papers scattered on a table. It is anything but trying to accept that the whole room is a flat out wreckage. Be that as it may, we don't exactly have the full picture. Whatever remains of the place could be perfect and immaculate. Be that as it may, our absence of point of view is keeping us from seeing the master plan.

Look for interchange points of view by approaching other individuals for their conclusions, remarks, and inputs. Get a comprehension of how they see the circumstance before you focus on coming up with your excuses.

Take Full Responsibility for Your Failures and Mistakes: Excuses are regularly made because we would prefer not to assume responsibility for our weaknesses. When we assume full responsibility for every one of our disappointments and mix-ups, we rapidly develop with certainty. Also, we feel engaged because life is never again based upon fortunes or favorable luck, but instead on our capacity to adequately adjust to the changing conditions that life tosses in our direction.

Learn from Past Experience: Rather than rationalizing, focus on gaining from this experience. Ask yourself:

• What would I have to gain from this experience?

• What has this experience shown me about myself, life and others?

• How would I be able to utilize this experience to improve the situation later on?

• What move might I be able to make right now that would enable me to make a stride toward this path?

Focus on Your Strengths: When making excuses, we frequently center around how insufficient and inadequate we are. This confines our concentration and uncovers the majority of our shortcomings. To counter this, we ought to instead focus on our qualities, specifically how to utilize those qualities to make the best of each circumstance.

CHAPTER 4

ACHIEVING GREATER SUCCESS

"Making the most of yourself for that is all there is of you" (Ralph Waldo Emerson).

I am a firm believer that to become a better person and achieving greatness; you first have to make sure that you love yourself, encourage yourself, speak life to yourself and practicing self-care. Growing up and as I can remember I have always learned from the mistakes and I am still learning even as an adult. I was always hard on myself while growing up. I always wanted to make sure that I was standing right as a person. I was still trying to become better in every area of my life either mentally, spiritually, cognitively, socially, financially and physically. If you want to continue to grow into the person you desire to be, the first thing you must do is to surround yourself with positive people, go-getters, loving people, and people that will hold you accountable for your actions to track the progress you are making consistently.

I learned that when you want to become a better person, you need to get real with yourself; you will need to stop blaming others for your actions, holding on to un-forgiveness, allowing fears of your past and present to hold you back. You need to learn how to cope with all these different emotions through fasting, meditation, music, join a support group organization, reading self-help books and just releasing what you are feeling through writing on a daily journey. I found this to be a valuable tool, and you will see a great result but, whichever one you decide to choose, you have to stick with it so you can develop into the person you desire to be.

I now understand that through all the storms that I had the experience, I really needed to be honest with myself in order to see results and through the whole process from a child and up till now how vital taking care of yourself is crucial and taking the time out to take care of yourself on a daily basis. I had to understand that to be a better person whether spiritually, naturally, personally or professionally. I feel you always need to hold and speak the truth. I think that's how you also can become a better person. I learned that when you help someone else, you are also helping yourself and developing into the person you needed to be. I found this to be very useful in becoming a better person when you are supportive and helping others who might be in worst shape as you are helping yourself from becoming that person. I can remember when I was going through my storms to improve myself better and transforming into this unique, incredible person, and I had to realize how vital it is to take care of your personal need. That was when I began to help all the people that I came in contact with whether it was on a daily, weekly or monthly basis. According to (Mohands Gandhi) "Be the change you wish to see in the world."

It is essential that you learned to be yourself. We live in a world where people want to be everybody, but not their true self. We have to be able to align ourselves and make sure we are forming our own identity because it is straightforward to try to steal someone else identity. This is something I struggle with until I start discovering my true authentic self. The fact is that it doesn't happen overnight, and it is a process, but the process is right for you. Anything is possible when you believe you can achieve what you are set out to achieve.

No matter how hard life may seem, how much things must have gone wrong and the regrets that will linger at the back-end of your mind, you still need to dare for more. I'm pretty sure I was not the first teenage girl to get pregnant out of wedlock, and even more convinced I wasn't the last. So, to an extent, it's no big deal, at least to others outside my family circle. The real biggie was to move on and be a better person for myself and my child. It was the only thing I thought to do, and today I am proud I made that decision.

Even when my family started to see me differently and neglecting me, I still found a reason to move and achieve greater success. I wasn't all for the "It's all over for me" mentality. Looking back on it now, I found some habits I cultivated to see me through the phase and be the person writing this book today. It would be best if you practiced this thing:

Gratefulness

It doesn't help when you wake up each morning and do nothing but complain of the many tasks you have on your desk, just as it isn't the right move to remember the bad events that happen the previous day, week or month. There is a reason they are called "past." What you need to do is be grateful for what you have, let go of what you can't, chase your dreams. Be happy you get another day of life, for the littlest and biggest possible things you have including love, abilities, a healthy body, food to eat, luxuries and facilities at your disposal. If you have anything significant in your possession it's what others may not have; then you have every reason to be grateful. Be proud of yourself and make it a religion always to be so. Start your days on a good note and the rest great stuff will naturally follow.

Be Yourself

I hear most people; especially women, get carried away with the greener-looking pastures on the other side and decide to make it a pain-bringer to cross over. Life is indeed not a competition. In spite of affluence and poverty, we all live and die. It is a natural, endless cycle of us all being the same. So, whomever you might be, that is who you are. The minute you start trying to be someone else, you are losing yourself already. The best person you can be is you. However, that doesn't mean you don't find out about your ugly side and try to keep it from getting in the way of your success. You can, of course, emulate the useful or promising features of successful people. You can start reading books, hitting the gym, joining support groups and setting up your own business. In as much as you are putting some generic tips out there into your employ, you should still retain the most of yourself, the one that makes you different.

Move On

Past bitterness will only draw you back from achieving your goals. If you let them hold you for too long, they will eat you up until you lose a grip of yourself and go into phase. Rather than sulking, wallowing, regretting and reflecting on the fine glass bits life has thrown at you, dust the earth from your feet and tell yourself it's about the future and not the past or present. Learn to let things go. A boy dumped you because he felt you are up to no good? Move on and get something of more value going on for yourself. If it helps, think about the unpleasant experiences in detail for one last time, take a deep breath and mentally move past them. It will make you feel lighter and stronger to do higher.

Look Ahead

After deciding a fresh start for yourself, make it a religion always to have a vision of whom you want to be in the next year and the next 365 days after that. Don't be dragged back, but plan for the future and press forward.

You are only as good as you see yourself to be. Learn to separate yourself from the things that affect your sanity. If you have to face your fears to overcome them, then do your best to beat that beast.

CHAPTER 5

WOMEN SHOULD SUPPORT EACH OTHER

I need you. You need me. We all are part of the great plan. You are

important to me. I need you to survive.

As I can remember I have always been a great supporter of women helping each other, in spite of the experience of life challenges and situations that I had found myself in. I have always had the heart to serve other women in all their endeavors and in any other way that I can and still doing it to this day. We live in a selfish world where everyone is only concerned about themselves. However, I am so grateful for the heart God has given me to learn how to help, encourage, push and empower other women from all walks of life, race and various background to become that incredible woman. I am so ever grateful to make an impact in the life of other women. I know when you support other women, it is not only uplifting you, but it will help both of you reach your destined goals. I know that by supporting each other, you also can share ideas, thoughts and still learn ways to empower each other whether it be on a daily, weekly or monthly basis. You are also setting a positive example to those egocentric women on how vital it is to work together than be competitive. When we work together, I also feel we can fulfill our destiny faster because two heads are better than one. As I was going through my challenges in life, I was grateful to have strong supportive women who stood by me and who held me accountable. There is no need to be jealous, envious or in competition; this only slows down the life process of the women you connect with, either personally or professionally.

I have always pushed other women as long as I can remember as a little girl growing up and up to my adult life. I remember encouraging them not to give up on their dreams and vision. I always support them to be all that they can be so they could reach their God giving full potential; I had always shared with women's from all walks of life and various backgrounds that it is never too late to pursue their goals, dreams, and education. So many women's failed to realize just because you had kids and some setback or even getting up in age you are never too old to finish school and to live out your destiny. That's why I think it's essential to join a women group at work and school because you can bounce off of each other especially when you are at your lowest. It is good to have women's there that you know whom it can ease up the process a little bit quicker.

As women, I know the sacrifice we have to make because often we wear so many hats in the home, from being a mom to being a coach team player, a friend, help with homework and wife the list can go on and on. I was always blessed for having my support system my significant other Johnny L.H. who was always there to support me in any way that he could and who stood by me through thick and then the storms and rain and my mom Judy.B who has always been there from day one and still is to this very day. I can remember my mom saying to me "I understand you are having a baby at a young age, but you will finish school and graduate" and that was a fact and she meant just what she said. I did graduate at the age of seventeen. Having God and a strong positive networking women's whom you can rub shoulders with is beautiful when facing tough times in your life.

I can remember a time when I was in school and felt like giving up and had gotten to the very end of my journey, it was about a month and a half to graduation, I felt like it was too much and I don't have the courage nor strength to get through all this school work. Mind you working a full-time Job, five kids and other obligations that needed to be fulfilled daily. I was so grateful for my two friends and Professor who also played a remarkable role in my success, and they are all women. I connected and built a positive relationship with two of my classmates whose names were 'Cynthia and Ms. Green' they encourage me to hold on and to lift my head and said: "we will get through this rough time." I thank God for them believing in me, and I held on in there and completed my course and graduated with my Master Degree in spite of the stumbling blocks on my way. That is why we have to realize how important working together is and realize that we all have our unique journey and with God and a positive support team of authentic and compassionate women we can conquer.

I believe that we can all do better. Women need to embrace intersectional feminism, the knowledge of how the overlapping identities of women, including race, class, ethnicity, religion and sexual orientation among others, impact the way they experience oppression and discrimination. We have to come to term with these if we are ever going to move the needle forward toward equal rights. According to Maya Angelou, "I love to see a young girl go out and grab the world by the lapels.

While there are so many ways women can support each other, I think the major problem is that we often fail in our duties. Between women, there is always an iota of jealousy, rivalry, or envy ongoing, but we could try to make our lives so much easier if we would get out of each other's way. Supporting others doesn't only mean showing compassion, but it's as well vital to remember that we can learn from each other every single day that comes and passes. Additionally, supporting each other in difficult times is one beautiful gesture, but to be there for each other when things are going well is also essential. Here are some ways we can support each other through thick and thin.

Be Happy For Other Women

We often fail to be happy for one another and may come to share in the pain when all goes south. Like I said, supporting should exist in good times and in bad. Not being happy or not finding joy in each other's happiness is indeed indexed not the way to go. Take, for example, your girlfriend is in a relationship with the cutest guy ever, has the most fantastic job and a slim figure you would give anything to have. Not only is it un-nice to resent such a person because she has what you don't, but it is also an act of jealousy. If you deemed someone good enough to be your girlfriend, then that means she is good enough to deserve whatever it is that she has and whatever good that comes her way. It's basic logic, not rocket science. So the next time your best friend expresses her joy regarding a good happening in her life, tell and show how equally or unequally happy you are. Let her know she deserves it, and that you only wish such good fortune would come to you. If you aren't happy for your friends and loved ones, you will not find happiness, and good things certainly will not happen your way. It's called karma. As women, when our female friends get married, give birth, lands a job or wins an award, it is your duty as a bosom friend to be share in their happiness.

Stick Up for Other Women

If you are looking for a great way to support other women out there, then you should try to always stick up for them. This can be done in many ways. It could be donating money to women support foundations, volunteering membership for women support groups or religiously advocating. There are people out there you haven't met who can benefit a lot from the support you do from your home or office. Some women want to start their businesses but do not have sufficient funds to do so. Your donations for these people could go a long way to empower them to do more and become the game changers, especially in third-world countries. A more straight forward approach is just more up your alley. Also, you can support by defending one another both in private life and in public places such as the office, place of worship, park, museum or movie theater. You shouldn't just pass by when you see a man trying to harass a woman in a dinging elevator sexually. You shouldn't just sit down and watch while a random lady is being denied her rights because she is a woman. Gender discrimination is a disease that needs to be wiped out of society, and that will take the actions of you and me to do it. Don't be too afraid to speak up for your friend when she cannot find her voice. If you notice a lady is not doing a good job to defend herself from being bullied probably because she is outnumbered, make it a duty to swoop in and save the day or call for help. Don't just turn your face away with the mindset that it is not your business. The young females need to be supported too through life. They are the ones who need it the most. Teach them how to dress and act cordially in public, so they don't put themselves in dangerous situations. Talk to them about basic etiquette, not just about the dos and don'ts. They need to hear it from you that they are not just ordinary people but set aside to impact the world positively. Stick up for her. Is she going through a financial phase that's not letting her afford the basic stuff? Lend her some money. Is she too sick she cannot cook for herself and family? Try to finish up early from work and prepare them some good food. We have not truly lived until we do something for others, what they may not be able to repay us for. As Saint Augustine rightly says, "The true essence of living is for others." Women from all over the world should stick up for each other, even online. Is someone posting an article on social media that demoralized a woman? Act against it, stand up for that woman no matter what, because nobody is perfect and as such has no right to be the judge over anything and everything. While the rest of the world are looking for whom to criticize, troll or use as a laughing stock, be the unbreech, the bigger women and every lady's knight in shining armor. If we learn to stick up for each other, the world will become a better place for not just women, but everyone else. If this continues, we would be looking at years to come without much strife, disagreement, pains, regrets and everything else seemingly odd. As the saying goes, "Divided we fall, but united we will stand."

Be Extra Welcoming

If a new lady joins your office, gym or apartment building, you can go out of your way to be welcoming. No, it's not poking around prying. It's making sure that the person gets comfortable as soon and as easy as possible. Other women should warmly receive the woman joining your group, and you can all understand her a gift to make it more memorable. After that, you can ask her out for lunch sometimes or ask to see a movie with her. It doesn't have to be every time. Even if it is once in a month, it would mean a lot to the other person. Some men love to prey on new women around an environment, just because they are less experienced regarding the way things go around. It is your job as a fellow, supportive woman to let the new lady know of these potential threats and warn them to stay off their paths. If there was anything which must have been a major or minor setback for you, suggest to them the best way to get around it. Let them know the best grocery store to go shopping, the coolest park, the most exciting movie theater or the newest gym to hit to get those muscles tight. Welcoming a modern woman means you are telling her everything you know about the environment and making sure they get comfy real soon. When they come to you with questions, even in your busiest moments, try to find time to give generic answers and advice.

Be Each Other's Plus One

This one is for the team. Sometimes, you may walk into a business class, an office environment, a gym or any other place filled with people only to find out there is testosterone domination in the arena. It may feel like walking into a death trap sometimes, but it shouldn't, not when you have a woman by your side. Being a plus one to another woman means forming a tea, with her and overcoming the challenges which females are likely to face. Like I said, this one for the team. There is no gainsaying that women are made for one another, amongst other things. Women writers, motivational speakers, actors, bloggers, and enthusiasts are out to preserve the dignity of womanhood nowadays. It is now up to you and me to form a strong alliance at the grass root and make sure that all other women gain from the collective energy. If your friend is interested in trying out activity, taking that class or going to that place where tends to be dominated by men, you can offer to go with her. You never know, it could just be the one thing that will give her the courage to go. Moreover, that resolution could ultimately be the life-changing decision for that lady. If you have a part to play in the success of another woman, it's a noble deed which every woman in the world would want to emulate.

I had always wanted to play a vital role in making an essential difference in young teens, young women and older women lives an creating a more joyful, peaceful life whether it be one on one, group session, conference, phone, event or just meeting up for lunch and the list can go on and on. I feel that I made a huge difference in the lives of women in my community.

As women around the world are making a significant difference and I am so proud to be a part of this same movement in my journey. I always made a difference in women lives from all walks of life whether it be to motivate, empower, support and mentally, spiritually and have made a massive transformation in their lives as well as myself. I genuinely believe that for you to make a difference in someone else life, you first have to start with your own life so you can help shape, mold and transform another human being life.

As a woman of God, mother, friend, mentor, and coach. I have made a tremendous difference in the lives of women that may struggle with who they are, and if I did not conquer my confidence, identity crisis, I would not have been able to make a difference in other women's lives. There was a time that I did not believe in myself I try everything to cover and hid behind whether it be a false image or pretending to be something that you are not and this is so easy to do, but with all that said in done when you return to the true self you still fill empty. I did not realize how it was keeping me back from begging my true Authentic self. We live in a world that full of young and old women trying to make a difference in others' lives and have not even made a difference in their own life you have to help yourself before you can go out to stabilize and make a difference in the life of others. I now discover and realize when you live a false identity, it can hold you back from becoming your true self, dreams, goals and all the promise you have locked inside of you.

My goal has always wanted to make a difference and ensure that as I connect with other women, it brings joy, peace, happiness, support and so much more. When creating a difference, it takes a lot of courage and a positive outlook on life because, so many people come from various walks of life and have a different experience in life, so we have to be very mindful of our approach when we are making a difference in others life. The same transformation that it took for me, I want to help to see and transform women lives and how I can indeed make a difference in their lives. I have seeing result in other women lives that I have mentored and coach along with my journey, but after working with these women, they first had to want to make the change. I know to make any change or difference sometimes it can be challenging to work with women because at some time we can become too emotional negative mindsets, thoughts, etc. I now realized making a difference is much need in this society that we are currently living in so many women are battling depression, hurt, rejection, disappointment, fail dreams and want to give up on life. I said if I am going to make a difference as Women, I have to lead by example and start making a difference in my own life on a daily and consistent basis.

CONCLUSION

Life isn't fairytale, and we all know that, however, it's the most precious gift that human received, and we need to take care of that gem. Every one of us has a dream, we all have a mission on this earth, and everyone was born with a purpose that can be painted into a more beautiful future if we allow ourselves to walk the path of our own life's story.

I had always to remind myself when it comes for me to be incredible, I had to really understand that in order for me to develop into an incredible woman, I had to make sure I was not imitating someone else's identity, style, either trying to talk like someone, various hairstyles, dressing, acting and so on. If you want to be that incredible authentic person, you have to learn how to embrace your unique qualities and to tell yourself and recognize how wonderful you are and there is no one like you.

After going through storms and growing into that incredible women within me. I had to make sure I was developing after battling all the storms of life having great interpersonal skill when you have a positive outlook on life, it is then when you will start building and attracting incredible people just like you who possessed the same abilities as you, create healthy, confident, positive and significant relationships is very vital. Incredible people influence to make anyone feel safe. I remember the time I can be in the store and start talking to someone who might be having a bad day, but being the incredible women help me uplift the person that might feel like giving up on life. You have to love people, be kind, respectful, understanding these qualities will carry you a long way than your gifts and talent and love is everything and people will never forget how you made them feel rather than what you said out of your mouth. It's two different things: love is an action word, and at all times it is essential that as you are becoming this incredible one, you are first discovering the incredible women in you.

TO BE CONTINUED!

28